THE VICAR OF NIBBLESWICKE

PUFFIN BOOKS

The Reverend Lee is worried about being in charge of his own parish for the first time. Will he be able to cope with all the responsibility of weddings, funerals, the choir, the bell-ringers and, above all, the sermons at Nibbleswicke? So worried is he that the dyslexia from which he suffered as a child comes back, in the form of a strange speech defect. He doesn't realize he's doing it, but key words come out of his mouth backwards, and thus, for example, he is apt to give his congregation 'the blessing of Dog Almighty'.

The parishioners are amused and later shocked at the garbled messages coming from the pulpit until finally a cure is found: the Vicar of Nibbleswicke must walk backwards for the rest of his life.

The Vicar of Nibbleswicke was written by Roald Dahl in the last months of his life. In a typical act of generosity he donated the story (and Quentin Blake the illustrations) for the benefit of the Dyslexia Institute. In a foreword to *The Vicar of Nibbleswicke*, Quentin Blake describes his work with Roald Dahl, and the way in which this book came to be written.

THE VICAR OF NIBBLESWICKE

ROALD DAHL

ILLUSTRATED BY
QUENTIN BLAKE

PUFFIN BOOKS

PUFFIN BOOKS
Published by the Penguin Group
Penguin Books USA Inc., 375 Hudson Street, New York, New York 10014, U.S.A.
Penguin Books Ltd, 27 Wrights Lane, London W8 5TZ, England
Penguin Books Australia Ltd, Ringwood, Victoria, Australia
Penguin Books Canada Ltd, 10 Alcorn Avenue, Toronto, Ontario, Canada M4V 3B2
Penguin Books (N.Z.) Ltd, 182–190 Wairau Road, Auckland 10, New Zealand

Penguin Books Ltd, Registered Offices: Harmondsworth, Middlesex, England

First published in Great Britain by Random Century Group Ltd, 1991
First published in the United States of America by Viking Penguin,
a division of Penguin USA Inc., 1992
Published in Puffin Books, 1993

1 3 5 7 9 10 8 6 4 2

ISBN 0-14-03 6837-X
Printed in the United States of America

FOREWORD

When I first, at the invitation of Tom Maschler of
Jonathan Cape, produced a set of sample drawings for
Roald Dahl's book *The Enormous Crocodile,* it had not
occurred to me – I don't think it had occurred to any of
us – that we were embarking on a collaboration that
would extend over fifteen years and a dozen books. It's
a collaboration of which I am proud and of which I
have a lot of memories.

Memories, of course, of discussion of pictures, of the
subjects for pictures, of the interpretation of characters;
most often carried out in the sympathetic atmosphere of
Gipsy House, in the midst of the Dahl family. But other
associated memories too, such as those Christmas
readings which Roald used to give at the National
Theatre. His audience filled one of the great
auditoriums – the Lyttleton or the Olivier – but
nevertheless Roald, rooting in his old leather brief-case
for the pages of an as yet unpublished story, seemed
perfectly at ease; perfectly able to talk as though he
were talking to each person individually. And, after the
performance, the signing of books. No children's author
can surely have signed as many books as Roald Dahl:
the queue at the National Theatre would be across the
foyer and down the stairs; and though it might take two

hours, everyone had a word and a signature. This concern for his readers and readiness to be available to them didn't end there. There were, for instance, replies to thousands of letters, both to children and teachers, with specially-written poems regularly renewed; and endless visits to schools and libraries.

And as well as generosity with time there were other kinds of generosity, works and gifts for charities and other institutions. They were private, not much talked about. But Roald had asked me to assist him in one or two projects for charity – a Christmas card for Great Ormond Street Hospital, for instance – and so it wasn't altogether a surprise to hear that familiar voice on the telephone, early last year, asking me if I'd be prepared to illustrate something that he was writing for the Dyslexia Institute. What *was* surprising was to hear what was being offered: the auction of all rights, world-wide, for the period of copyright. It's a privilege to be associated, among our many collaborations, with Roald in this book; a landmark of both his concern for people and his passionate belief in the importance of reading.

1991

Once upon a time there lived in England a charming and God-fearing vicar called the Reverend Lee. When as a young man he first came to take up his duties in the small village of Nibbleswicke, there was for a while utter confusion and often genuine consternation among his devout parishioners.

What had happened was this: as a boy, Robert Lee had suffered from severe dyslexia. However, guided by the Dyslexia Institute in London and helped by some excellent teachers, Robert made such splendid progress that by the time he was eighteen his writing and reading were both more or less normal and he was able to gratify his ambition to go into training for the ministry.

All went well and by the time he was twenty-seven Robert Lee had become the Reverend Lee and had been appointed to his first important job as Vicar of Nibbleswicke.

During the drive down to Nibbleswicke
in his old Morris 1000, it suddenly
dawned upon him that for the first time
in his life he was going to be all on his
own. He began to get nervous. Would
he be equal to running a parish? The
previous vicar, as he knew, had died in
harness and there would be nobody
there to guide him.

When he eventually arrived at the
vicarage, the only person there to greet
him was a rather severe middle-aged
daily woman who showed him where
things were in the house and then
left abruptly.

Oh dear, thought poor Robert Lee as
he lay in bed that night trying to sleep.
*Will I really be able to cope with
this job?* Weddings, funerals,
christenings, Sunday Schools, the
organist, the verger, the church
committee, the choir, the bell-ringers
and, above all, the dreaded sermons . . .
His mind whirled. He began to sweat.

And it is clear now that sometime during that horrible night something must have gone *click* in his brain and stirred up in some way vestiges of the old dyslexia that was lying there dormant, because the next morning when he got up he was suffering, although he did not know it himself at the time, from a very peculiar illness. It wasn't dyslexia, but it was clearly related in some way to those old dyslexic problems. The way it affected him was as follows:

He would be talking to somebody and

suddenly his mind would subconsciously pick out the most significant word in the sentence and reverse it. By that I mean he would automatically spell the word backwards and speak it in that way without even noticing what he had done. For example: trap became part, drab became bard, God became dog, spirit became tirips and so on. I repeat that he was not aware of what he was doing and therefore he never thought to correct himself.

When the Reverend Lee got up on that first morning, he found a note left by the verger on his desk politely suggesting that he make a start in his new parish by calling right away upon the wealthiest and most fervent supporter of the church in Nibbleswicke. This, the note added, was a maiden lady by the name of Miss Arabella Prewt. Miss Prewt had recently footed the bill for one hundred new hassocks for the church, each one filled with sponge rubber, which was very easy on the knees, and the verger hinted that if the vicar played his cards right, the lady might be good for an even larger donation in the near future.

Very well, the Reverend Lee told himself, *I'd better call on Miss Prewt right away*; and he decided, so as to appear more friendly and informal, to leave off his dog-collar and to dress in mufti.

Setting off on foot, he soon found Miss Prewt's large Edwardian house, which was called 'The Haven', and he rang the bell. The door was opened by Miss Prewt herself, a tall, thin female who stood bolt upright and whose mouth was like the blade of a knife.

'My dear Miss Twerp!' cried the
Reverend Lee. 'I am your new rotsap!
My name is Eel, Robert Eel.'

A small black and white dog appeared
between Miss Prewt's legs and began to
growl. The Reverend Lee bent down
and smiled at the dog. 'Good god,' he
said. 'Good little god.'

'Are you mad?' shouted Miss Prewt. 'Who are you and what do you want?'

'I am Eel, Miss Twerp!' cried the vicar, extending his hand. 'I am the new rotsap, the new raciv of Nibbleswicke! Dog help me!'

Miss Prewt slammed the door in his face.

Things went from bad to worse. Soon the entire village was convinced that the new vicar was completely barmy. Pleasant and harmless, they said, but completely and utterly barmy.

On one occasion the Reverend Lee walked into the village hall, where the local ladies were holding their weekly knitting session, knitting sweaters for sailors in the Merchant Navy.

'How lovely!' he cried. 'How clever you all are! Each of you stink!'

Matters came to a head on the following Saturday when the Reverend Lee met a small group of women who he was supposed to be preparing for their First Communion.

'The only thing I'm not sure about,' said Mrs Purgativa, 'is whether you are supposed actually to *drink* the wine when the chalice is offered to you. If so, how much should one drink? What I mean is, should it be a good gulp or just a little sip?'

'Dear lady,' cried the vicar, 'you must never plug it! If everyone were to plug it the cup would be empty after about four goes and the rest of you wouldn't get any at all! What you must do is pis. Pis gently. All of you, all the way along the rail must pis, pis, pis. Do you understand what I mean?'

They didn't, and the meeting broke up in disorder. Yet the Reverend Lee was too nice and gentle a man for anyone to bear any deep malice towards him. They couldn't believe he was being deliberately obscene. There was something wrong somewhere but none of them could say what it was.

Then came the first Sunday morning
service, a great occasion for the village
and a greater one for the vicar. The
service turned out to be an amusing
business because the vicar kept
peppering his sentences with the most
extraordinary words. They weren't
obscene, nor did these words turn
themselves into other words that meant
anything at all; except in the case of one
or two, like 'dog' for 'God'. Very few
words *do* make sense when spelt
backwards, and the result of this was

that the nervous young man got away with it. In fact, most of the congregation found the zany word-crazy service a rather welcome change from the old routine of well-worn phrases. It was rather fun for instance to hear him intoning 'and forgive us our sessapsert, as we forgive those that ssapsert against us' rather than the other old thing. So on the whole the service went well and was voted very jolly indeed. Everyone was pleased with the new eccentric young vicar.

Then came the bombshell. When the service was over and 'the blessing of Dog Almighty' had been given, the vicar stepped forward to the front of the altar rail and spoke as follows:

'Dear people, it is hardly my place as a
newcomer to start making rules so early
in my incumbency, but there is just one
thing I feel I must mention. The road
outside our little church is exceedingly
narrow and, as you know, there is
hardly room for two vehicles to pass
each other. Therefore I feel it only right
to ask members of the congregation not

to krap all along the front of the church before the service. It is not only unsightly but it is also dangerous. If you all krap at the same time all along the side of the road you could be hit by a passing car at any time. There is plenty of room for you to do this alongside the church on the south side if you feel you must.'

The silence that greeted this announcement was like the end of the world and the poor vicar walked out of the church with not one kindly eye looking up to meet his.

In the end it was the local doctor who guessed what was wrong. 'What you've got,' he said, 'is a very rare disease called Back-to-Front Dyslexia. It is very common among tortoises, who even reverse their own name and call themselves esio trots. Fortunately,' went on the good doctor, 'there is a simple cure.'

'Tell me!' cried the vicar. 'Oh please tell me!'

'You must walk backwards while you are speaking, then these back-to-front words will come out frontwards or the right way round. It's common sense.'

The cure worked miraculously. There were problems, of course. The main one was that the poor chap couldn't see where he was going without twisting his head over his shoulder, which was painful. But by attaching a small rear-view mirror to his forehead with an elastic band, he overcame this difficulty.

Sermons were also awkward, but the congregation very soon grew accustomed to seeing their vicar walking backwards round and round the pulpit while he was preaching. In fact, it added a nice crazy touch to what was normally a dreary proceeding.

In the end, the Reverend Robert Lee got so good at walking backwards that he never walked forwards at all, and for the rest of his life he became a lovable eccentric and a pillar of the parish.

The Vicar of Nibbleswicke

ROALD DAHL was one of the greatest story-tellers of all time. He was born in Llanduff, South Wales, of Norwegian parents, in 1916, and educated in English boarding-schools. Then, in search of adventure, the young Dahl took a job with Shell Oil in Africa. When World War II broke out he joined the RAF as a fighter pilot, receiving terrible injuries and almost dying in a plane crash in 1942.

It was following this 'monumental bash on the head' and a meeting with C.S. Forester (author of the famous Captain Horatio Hornblower stories) that Roald Dahl's writing career began, with articles for magazines such as *The New Yorker*. He wrote successful novellas and short stories for adults, such as *Tales of the Unexpected*, before concentrating on his marvellous children's stories. The first of these, *James and the Giant Peach*, in 1960, was followed by *Charlie and the Chocolate Factory*, and an unbroken string of hugely successful, bestselling titles.

Roald Dahl worked from a tiny hut in the apple orchard of the Georgian house in Great Missenden, Buckinghamshire which he shared with his wife, Liccy. He was always brimming with new ideas and his many books continue to bring enormous enjoyment to millions of children and their parents throughout the world.

Roald Dahl died on 23 November 1990.

QUENTIN BLAKE, one of Britain's most renowned cartoonists and illustrators, was born in the suburbs of London. He began his career working for various magazines such as *The Spectator* and *Punch*. His genius for illustration and sharp eye for humorous detail led him into the world of children's books, where he is internationally known and loved for both his own picture books and his collaborations with other authors. The creative relationship between Quentin Blake and Roald Dahl in particular was a very special and enduring one – Blake's interpretation of Dahl's characters have become an essential part of childhood.

He was the Head of the Illustration Department at the Royal College of Art from 1978 to 1986 and is now visiting Professor. He was awarded the OBE in 1987.

With a few deft, instantly recognizable, strokes of the pen, Quentin Blake can bring any character or situation hilariously to life. His spell is irresistible.

And for adults

THE BEST OF ROALD DAHL
COMPLETELY UNEXPECTED TALES
KISS, KISS
MORE TALES OF THE UNEXPECTED
MY UNCLE OSWALD
OVER TO YOU
SOMEONE LIKE YOU
SWITCH BITCH
TALES OF THE UNEXPECTED